1

᛫ᚠᛟᚱ᛫ᛟᚢᚱ᛫ᚠᚢᛏᚢᚱᛗ᛫ᚦᛗ᛫ᚲᛁᚾᛞᛗᚱᚠᛟᛚᚲ᛫

FOR OUR FUTURE:
OUR Children

᛫ᚠᛟᚱ᛫ᛟᚢᚱ᛫ᚠᚢᛏᚢᚱᛗ᛫ᚦᛗ᛫ᚲᛁᚾᛞᛗᚱᚠᛟᛚᚲ᛫

Vivienne

Grandpa + Granma
Marr
Christmas 2013

KINDERTALES

More Stories for the Children of the Folk

Kindertales II: More Stories for the Children of the Folk

Thor's Troll-Goat; The Lay of Goldenlocks and the Three Bears; Vargus the Vegetarian Troll; Wolf and Wyrd: Of Fenris and the Hand; Draugr of Hudiksrall; The Story of Mistletoe © John Mainer
Gifts; Snjóa © Freydis Heimdallson
Interior Art © Freydis Heimdallson
Edited by Freydis Heimdallson
Cover Art and Design © Freydis Heimdallson

Proceeds from the sale of this book to benefit the non-profit Heathen Freehold Society of British Columbia.

ISBN 978-0-557-94175-9

Visit us online at http://bc-freehold.org

Published by
The Freyr's Press
Heathen Freehold Society

TABLE OF CONTENTS

ᚠᛟᚱ·ᛟᚢᚱ·ᚠᚨᛏᚢᚱᛖ·ᚦᛖ·ᚲᛁᚾᛞᛖᚱᚠᛟᛚᚲ·

ᚠᛟᚱ·ᛟᚢᚱ·ᚠᚨᛏᚢᚱᛖ·ᚦᛖ·ᚲᛁᚾᛞᛖᚱᚠᛟᛚᚲ·

Thor's Troll-Goat, or The Day the Goats Rode

By John Mainer

Thor was riding his great chariot towards Jottunheim; his two goats Tanngrisni ("Gap-tooth") and Tanngnost ("Tooth Gnasher") drove him onward like thunder. Thor had heard that Thrym, the frost giant jarl, was planning on raiding into Midgard, and the land of Men was under Thor's protection.

As he rode, his iron gauntlet was on the haft of his strong hammer, Mjolner, for Jottunheim was filled with dangers, and even a god must ride wary. As he came to the bridge at Skullford, his goats snorted a warning. Tooth Gnasher growled, and Gap-tooth gave a chuckling snort: they smelled troll.

Trolls were a common problem in Jottunheim, haunting many bridges, the dark mountain passes, and the forgotten forest glens. Trolls commonly struck from hiding, for although fierce, they were not terribly brave. Thor readied his hammer and rode boldly forward into the troll's trap. With a growling roar the troll jumped onto the bridge behind Thor.

"GOAT!" roared the troll, as he jumped on the bridge.

"TROLL!" cheered Thor, as his hammer swung.

"Noooooooooo!" wailed the troll, as he started to cry. "Not fair, not fair, not fair!" cried the troll as he curled up in a ball.

Thor's great hammer hung in mid air, a puzzled expression on his great shaggy head. The troll was naught but a child, and scrawny besides; not the weight of a good wooden shield. While Thor was the smiter of Giant and Troll, he was the protector of children as well.

"He promised two goats if I let him pass by, a goat for my own, just for me!" wailed the troll boy.

"Who promised?" asked Thor with a snarl.

"Loki himself, and he swore on his name!" wept the troll, as he sobbed and he shook.

Thor was no stranger to Loki's cruel jokes, and was moved to pity the troll child.

"Enough of your wailing, wee troll!" said Thor, laughing. "Hurry and get us a fire. An oath should be kept by a kinsmen, 'tis true, so it's a goat of your own just for you!"

As Thor unhitched his glossy goat team, did the little troll build them a fire. The eyes of the troll never left off Gap-Tooth, and he drooled with his starving desire. The fire was laid, and the troll grew afraid; the goats eyed him with fearless aggression.

"O Thor, I'm afraid to touch your fierce goats; they look like they don't want to be eaten! Besides," spoke the troll, "If we eat them both up, who then will pull your mighty war-chariot?"

"Hah!" laughed bold Thor. "My goats fear no troll; but my goats are magic, you see. Each night can I kill them, and eat them both up, and each morning they spring forth anew!"

Thor struck as he spoke, and brained both his goats; Tooth Gnasher, and Gap-Tooth were fallen. Neither goat seemed shocked or offended.

"When we're done, we toss the bones on the skin, and tomorrow they're both good as new!"

Thor sat and relaxed as the troll got to work, amused at his happy babbling troll nonsense.

"Promise me, boy, you will not touch the bones or the skin, or I'll make you replace them!"

"I promise, O Thor," spoke the hungry troll child. "I promise, I promise, I promise!"

As the goats turned on spits the troll boy was drooling; these goats were like nothing he'd eaten. He dreamed of the rich flesh, the dripping hot fat; but he dreamed too of golden goat marrow. Cracking and sucking the marrow of bones was a troll boy's deepest desire.

10

Try as he might to keep his troll oath, his stomach was always the winner. When Thor was busy collecting his bones, the troll cracked one juicy leg bone, and sucked it all up!

When Thor turned around, he tossed it quickly onto the skin, and thanked Thor for his generous feast.

Come the dawn, the poor troll awakened in flight. He awoke as he soared through the air. He was tossed on the horns of Tooth Gnasher the goat, while Thor yelled at the troll.

"You've lamed him, you nasty wee troll!"

Thor shook his great fists as his goat beat the troll. Gap-Tooth could not even stagger. One leg was clean broke from the marrow-sucking troll, and Gap-Tooth was lamed as a cripple.

Thor took up his hammer to settle the score; he aimed at the well-battered troll.

"I'll replace him!" the troll screamed as he was tossed by the goat. "I'll pull you until he gets better!"

"Hold, Tooth Gnasher!" spoke Thor in his thundering voice. "Let this troll learn the price of his actions."

Suiting actions to words Thor hitched up the troll, and tied Tooth Gnasher in place right beside him. "I've a giant to hunt down in Jottunheim."

Thor cracked the whip and Tooth Gnasher pulled, but the troll-boy tripped for a tumble.

Each time the pace changed the troll took a fall, and Tooth Gnasher did bite him. Soon the goats, god, and troll were battered and bruised, and not one mile had they gone.

"Enough!" roared Thor when the troll's next fall earned a nip. "You can't pull in a team; you're no fit match for my goat. You'll have to pull us alone."

Panting and sweating, grunting and groaning, the troll dragged the chariot through Jottunheim's

mountains. Thor and his goats rode in chuckling leisure; the goats in particular watched with great pleasure.

Deep in the pass by Svartafel Glacier, the swearing wee troll-goat slipped in the snow, and slid two bowshots under the chariot. Yelping his fear and scampering like a rabbit, the troll kept from squishing while taking a bashing.

From the deep drifts of snow came a chorus of chuckling. The veil of the magic broken with the silence, Thor saw the trap his chariot had brought him to.

Full two hundred giants were waiting in ambush; Thrym had brought all his brothers and clansmen. They were trapped in the pass where a single crack of loud thunder would bury bold Thor in the mountain's own ice. Knowing that throwing his hammer was out, Thor prepared to fight to the last.

His mighty chest filled for his mighty war cry, Thor choked in surprise as cries split the air.

"Please don't kill me! I've been a good troll; I don't want to die!"

The troll was on his knees begging the surrounding Frost Giants for mercy. The two goats were bleating and snorting their rage, for as their stand-in, the troll-goat was shaming them before their most ancient foe.

While the troll-goat, still hitched to the chariot was being butted and bleated at by the two goats, one of whom was limping badly, Thor himself now turned to the troll.

"Stand fast, you oath-breaking, leg-cracking, troll-smelling goat-boy! Today you are one of my goats, not a cowardly troll. You will face death with courage, with honour!"

As Thor shouted the troll sniveled louder and louder.

All around the waiting Frost Giants were laughing so hard they were falling down, and dropping their axes. One laughed so hard he dropped his spear, and watched it slide all the way down the mountain, which only made the other giants laugh harder.

Thyrm, mighty son of Ymir, Jarl of Frost Giants, and champion of Jottunheim, watched his ambush collapse into a joke, and his great plan for revenge slip away like his huscarl's lost spear. Watching the little troll beg, mighty Thor roar, and two angry goats bleat and poke at the cowering troll, Thrym realized that while many giants may have boasted to have faced Thor, and one or two even to have tricked him, only Thyrm could ever claim to have one of Thor's goats beg him for mercy, and if Thor's goat was a scrawny hill troll, that just made the boast better.

Laughing with the rumble of the breaking river ice, Thyrm ended the battle.

"Go in peace, mighty Thor, for we never planned harm to the world of men; simply to avenge your slaughter of giants!"

Thor, goats, and troll halted in surprise, having almost forgotten the towering giants.

"I swear by my father's name that I will take my men home, that we will raise no weapon more deadly than our drinking horns for a fortnight or more!"

Thyrm could get no farther, for he burst out laughing again, like the sound of boulders falling down a mountain side. "It will take that long to tire of telling everyone of Thor's "mighty" troll-goat!"

Moved to the generosity that made him a mighty chieftain among the giants, Thyrm gifted both true goats with silver torcs he bent around their proud necks himself. To Thor he gave a mighty Jottun-sized keg of good beer to wash down the taste of defeat, and lastly, he hung a golden ring from his mighty finger around the troll's neck like a thrall collar.

Thus it was that Thor returned to Asgard, walking beside his chariot.

All the gods and heroes stopped to gaze at the sight in wonder, as the silver-clad goats snorted and bleated, the scrawny hill troll bowed and beamed, and mighty Thor stumped along, drinking right from the keg.

To this day, Tooth Gnasher and Gap-Tooth will not pass any troll without thumping them.

The Lay of Goldenlocks and the Three Bears

By John Mainer

hear now the tale of Goldenlocks
The fair maiden who went to pick berries,
Became lost,
And entered legend!

Goldenlocks had been sent to pick berries for a guest,
A stranger claiming guest rights at her father's hall,
And Goldenlocks had always been told the laws
Three days the best of food and drink to receive.

Gone were the berries in easy reach
Her sisters had eaten the best
No lesser berries to a guest to serve,
So Goldenlocks onward pressed.

Deep in the bushes after berries she went

Onward and onward still

Lost in the maze of the bushes at dusk

Goldenlocks picked the whole day.

Stumbling in the dark as it began to rain

Goldenlocks started to cry

At last she came to a sheltering cave

Giving thanks to the gods for its warmth.

A fire was laid in the rear of the cave,

A stone table was set right before

Crude beds were set along the back of the walls

Yet neither tools nor weapons were hung.

Goldenlocks stumbled to the stone table's warmth

She gently picked up the first bowl

No spoons or knives could she find to help eat

So she grabbed a quick fingerful.

With a cry of despair she dropped the hot bowl

Too hot was the porridge to eat!

The next bowl she picked up and took a quick scoop,

Too cold; it was hard as a rock!

The last bowl was warm and she gobbled it down;

Once full and warm she got sleepy.

She stumbled towards the smallest of beds,

But she tripped and fell on its covers.

Smashed was the first bed,

She felt very sorry,

But even more tired was she;

Again and again did she strive.

Climbing the tallest again did she fail,

Just pulling the fur covers right off!

At last did she climb in the middle nest bed,

And pull the warm moose hides around.

So deep was her sleep that she missed the arrival

Of the family of great shaggy bears:

A little cub just the size of a hound,

But parents the size of two oxen!

"Someone has taken a bite of my porridge,"
Growled the father bear in swift-building fury
"Someone has taken a bite of mine too!"
Said the cub sounding clearly excited.

"Someone has taken *all* of *my* porridge,"
Said the mother in her rousing anger.
Goldenlocks mumbled still deep in her sleep
As the shaggy bears searched all around them.

"Someone has gone and broken my bed!"
Said the baby bear now getting angry.
Father bear looked at his furs on the ground:
"Someone has messed too with mine!"

Mother bear looked in her own bed to see
A golden-locked cub of a human
Sleeping curled up, not a care in the world,
With shaggy bears gathered around her.

Gently the mother bear poked the wee child;

With a smile she woke from her sleep.

"I am a traveller, and I claim my guest rights!"

Said the girl in tones of conviction.

She held out her basket of sweet new-picked berries;

"I come with this gift as guest-token."

The cub "ohhed" and "ahhed" at the smell of the

berries;

The bears looked around in confusion.

Hospitality laws were laid down by the gods,

But who knew that a human could use them?

With a shrug the mother bear took the basket of

berries.

"Be welcome, our guest, to our home."

Three days did the bears and the girl feast and play.

By day would the cub and the girl run and play;

By night did she do mother bear's nails.

Father bear looked at it all with wide wonder.

When three days were up there was not much to
ponder;
The honour of bears was demanding
No choice but to take wee Goldenlocks home
With the shaggy bears all her attending.

The cry from the searchers was brought to the hall
Where all her kinfolk had been searching:
Here strode Goldenlocks with three shaggy bears
To her hall and into her legend.

Vargus the Vegetarian Troll

By John Mainer

Bright Sunna wards the daytime sky; her touch is death to trolls. Only Yuletide's dark and endless night makes the daytime theirs to roam. Dokkalfar, draugr, and troll must ever to shadows keep, and only in the coming dark about the world to creep. So it was for age on age, and so it is today. I sing you now of a troll that dared to find another way.

Vinland was the land last found by the ancients' dragon-prowed ships. One day Vinland would birth two nations, but I speak of what first comes. Before our dragon crested ships, before pilgrims and fur trade, there came across the northern wastes a bridge that ice had made. Across this bridge there ran the herds, of reindeer and caribou. Running from the spears of men, there came the hill troll, too.

Far from the land of Norse and Dane, far from the Russ and Finn, the troll was hunted where e'er it fled by the mighty tribes of men. Across the fells a silence came, where once the troll did call; across the night a peace did reign, but peace did not come for all. In Vinland's north the troll had come against the tribes so poor. No iron spears to hunt the troll, nor stout walls to keep within. Wendigo they named the beast, and feared it all the night, till sons of Europe sailed again, to Vinland's forgotten shores.

Where once the troll had fled the spear, now they faced the gun. In a generation the trolls were hunted down, from the tundra and the plains.

Our story begins in truth with one, a troll that yet remains. Vargus, hill troll, orphaned young, is the hero of our tale. Parents slain by the mighty bear, who would rob them of their kill. Grandmother lost to the forest fire, leaving Vargus more bitter still.

Down to the town came the starveling troll, even to the homes of men. He would steal his meat from his ancient foes, and steal away again. He stole his way to the old folks' home, to the elders left alone. But Wyrd it seems can be weird indeed, for the troll was not alone.

By chance it seems, or by fate perhaps, was Vargus the hill troll caught. Not by warrior, hound, or trap did he fall. Not by bullet, blade, or spear. Vargus the hill troll was caught instead by a voice that rasped in his ears.

"You're late!" screeched a voice like a half scalded seagull. Behind him was truly a sight. "You promised to be here on this my birthday, and instead kept me waiting all night!"

Vargus was frozen in something like fear, for this woman had be-spelled him in truth. The woman was blinder than most wandering bats, but she'd still caught this poor troll youth. Not more than five feet, and bent like a bow, with a nose that could shame a fishhook. Warty of face, with a crone's hump besides, and naught but the one lonesome tooth, old granny was just like the grandma he'd lost, right down to the mean in her eye!

Vargus the lonely was caught in the spell, caught like a fly in the web. He'd come as a thief in the cold winters night; now he was invited within. The old woman was not prey to his fangs, for his heart she had conquered in truth. The words she had cast to strike her grandson, had instead caught this wild troll youth.

"Help your old granny with the door, boy!" The old woman demanded, and right quick did Vargus obey. He helped her to her easy chair, and set her feet upon the cushion. The old woman smiled, and offered the young troll a plate of fresh-baked meat pies, which the young troll munched on eagerly.

"I thought you had no time for your old granny and her silly stories about old times any more?" asked the mistaken old woman. "No time for tales of heroes and gods, trolls and wights."

Vargus was stunned so fiercely he stopped chewing (almost impossible in a starving troll). "Do you know stories about trolls?" asked Vargus.

"I know all the stories about trolls, from Grendel and his Mother, to Thor's chariot troll, to the Troll King's riddles," spoke the old woman with a cackle.

Vargus asked the questions that had burned inside him since he was a baby troll, and didn't have the words to ask his mother and grandmother before the bad winter and the bear took his family away.

Trolls as a tribe had lost their own lore, had forgotten what once they had known. Vargus himself held the anger inside, but the questions only had grown. In an instant the questions broke free of their bonds, questions of trolls and their plight. Three questions burst forth from the troll's broken heart, three questions that haunted him still:

"Why do the gods hate trolls? Why must trolls fear the sun? Who can a troll pray to?"

His pain and his heart in the old woman's lap, his soul in her hands to destroy. Vargus the troll watched the old woman pause, then gently she answered the boy.

"Bright Sunna the sun is the giver of life, and she hates those who prey upon man. None who will feast on the flesh of her tribe can stand in her light once again. Trolls pray to Jottun, the destroyers of life, whenever they bother at all. To Thyrum and the endless hunger of cold, and Surt and his devouring fire."

Vargus rode on the spell of her words, rode down the halls of the past. Cold and the hunger took mother and father, fire and smoke took his gran. No kinslayer spirit would get prayer from him; a pox on the Jottun entire!

"How could a troll make his peace with the gods?" asked Vargus with a tremble.

"By becoming a vegetarian!" laughed the old woman.

The heart of Vargus was transformed in an instant. He would make his peace with the gods, and join the tribe of this woman. Vargus the troll would be Vargus the Vegan!

As the winter progressed, Vargus did try. He ate only vegetables, and offered blot and symbel with his grandmother to the gods of her tribe. He offered strong oaths upon her family's own ring, to be vegetarian, and a loyal son of the tribe.

Oaths sworn to Sunna, to never eat man; oaths sworn to Frey, to touch no beast of flock or forest; oaths sworn to Frigga to be the truest of sons: all these were sworn on the oath ring at Yuletide. Sunna was stunned to be oathed by a troll, for her touch brings death to the dark and the troll. Frey laughed so loud that he startled his boar; only Frigga was silent as she witnessed the oath.

At the heart of the Yuletide he confessed his deception, admitted his trolldom to a startled grandmother. Rather than smite him, she touched him with wonder. Gnarled old hands touched his horned hide and muttered, "No son of my house to attend my old age, but a son from the fells who is not of my race.

"Attend me", she barked as she spat out her oath; "I claim this hill troll as my own grandson too.

"Vargus the Vegetarian, now son of my house."

Frigga spoke with a whisper that shattered the night: "The oath has been spoken by one with the right. The troll is now kindred, and owed our defence."

"Trolls must eat meat, or soon they will die," said Frey, whose own lordship claimed all beasts of the land. "He will soon be forsworn, or starved unto death."

"Until then," spoke Frigga, "Sunna must forefend."

A month past the Yuletide the troll and his gran were sitting and basking in the light of the sun. No more in the night was Vargus the Vegan bound to the dark like the trolls of past ages. Sitting and feeding the ducks with his granny, Vargus was starving and looking quite skinny. Full up with everything that he could eat, everything except the forbidden meat, Vargus was starving, for trolls, as you know, must eat of fresh meat or melt away like the snow.

Vargus was trembling, and weak at the knees when his eye fell on something he never had seen. In a house they walked past were two fat young men. They were caked with old food, and sunk deep in the couch. They were pale like a troll who'd not seen the sun, and soft like a custard that's started to run. The boys passed a pipe and puffed on it hard, and sat watching TV and turning to lard. They made Vargus drool like a wild hill troll, but he'd sworn off all meat when he took his new role.

"Couch potatoes," his grandmother said with a sneer. "They'd rather die, you see, then get off their rear."

Vargus was stunned, for he'd thought they were boys-- "Are you sure?" he asked Gran with a voice filled with hunger.

"Yes, I'm sure," said his gran, completing the blunder.

Later that night did the troll go to the drug den, and seek these potatoes that looked just like men. Mindful of his oaths he put to the test: were these real couch potatoes, or just men at rest? He asked of the first would he get up, or die? When told to "take off" he made this reply:

"I once was a troll and ate men and deer, but now I eat only couch potatoes, I fear. If you will not rise, then you are a potato, and with mayonnaise I will eat you on bagels!" The youth was too stoned to know this as truth, and thus was on multigrain fed to the tooth. The troll vegetarian had his misguided munching; the gods themselves became aware of his crunching.

Sunna determined to sear him at dawn, but Frey in his laughter bid her to hold on. Frigga herself was torn on the matter: an oath was an oath, but the wording does matter. To Tyr of the one hand they took the dispute. What should be done of the death of the youth?

The one-armed Lawgiver listened close to the oaths, and made his true judgement for the good of the folk. The boy did his best to hold to the truth, and thinking them vegetables ate this soft youth. Had the lad not been given to such shameful sloth, he would not have ended on troll tablecloth. The boy had become not a man but a pudding, and pudding and trolls can have only one ending.

Vargus the Vegetarian was granted reprieve. His oath was deemed honoured, and forgiven his feed.

Let all now bear witness to both lessons learned: take your kinsmen as found from whatever the source; and be sure to keep fit, or become the main course!

Wolf and Word: Of Fenris and the Hand

By John Mainer

At the dawn of the age of men did Odin swear blood-oath to Loki. Brothers they would be, that no cup be brought to the High One that did not Loki sip, that no hall would he raise that Loki not guest. Together with Thor they wandered the worlds, carving for mankind a place. Where strength alone could never win, did tricks and craft turn the tide. Thus Odin bound our world from the Jottun, with Loki ever by his side.

Where Odin gave his eye for sight, hung himself by noose and spear for knowledge, never did Loki look to change, and his tricks were as fair as foul. The Vanir and Aesir warded the earth, kept men from Jottun's old hunger, but Loki was ever of Jottun and god, never quite one or the other.

Two wives did Loki keep for himself, a goddess with children both fair, and a Jottun, Angrboda. Mother of Sorrows was Angrboda named, and her children by Loki were three. Hel the corpse-maiden fairest of these, while the serpent was with hatred most foul. Fenris the wolf was last of the three, his strength and his hunger ever growing.

At the root of Yggdrasil, the great World Tree, lies the Well of Wyrd, and the Norns. The three Norns it is that read of our fates, and speak of the dooms of us all. To Odin they spoke of the Trickster's Jottun kin, and the doom they promised for all. Thor and Tyr were sent for the brood, the hammer and sword of the folk. "Let the children of Loki be brought to this hall, for the High One to judge their fates."

Before the high seat were brought Angrboda's brood, before the gods in their judgement. Loki was swift to ward what was his, and with his tongue sought ever to ward them. Hel the corpse maiden was first to be seen. Half the shining white of a maiden, half the blood blue of a corpse; half goddess, half death hunger, she stood cold and silent, fearless before her god-kin. To Hel was then given Niflheim's dead. "Let the corpse maiden take them as hers. Let her raise her high hall in the land of the dead, and keep the corpse gate in her charge."

The serpent was writhing and hissing its hate, its venom it spewed at the gods. Thor with his hammer was rising to slay, when Loki did speak for his child.

"Blood brother I called you, now Kinslayer next. What host would so serve his own guest?

"If you fear him, then cast him where he can do you no harm!"

Heimdall saw doom in the life of the snake, Thor saw its hatred of all. Both joined their voices to demand the snake's death, but the All-Father by strong oaths was bound.

"Blood brother I swore at the birth of the worlds, and Hospitality Laws did I speak. Let the serpent be cast into the frothing cold sea; let it never to Asgard return."

Thor did raise up Mjollner's dark head and swear to the serpent itself, "If ever your venom is turned against man, if ever your fangs towards the gods, my hammer will make your swift end!"

Last of the brood was Fenris the wolf. As a pup he was the size of a grown hound. His grin was as fierce and his fangs knife sharp as the Wolf Lord's own dread wolves.

"Lord of the Wolves," Did Loki now beg, "I ask for the life of my son, for his is the hunger of battle alone. Can the Battle-glad doom Fenris for that?"

Frigg in her glory beseeched her dread lord to let the wolf be taken away. The stirrings of doom did she feel in the pup, the promise of endings to come.

No oath breaker Odin, though it cost him his all. Thus the Battle-glad gave his reprieve. "Let Fenris the wolf be guest in our lands, by our own sons with meat we will feed."

Thus sworn the High One sought to stay off the doom, to bind with ties forged of love. Let the wolf be a friend to both Gods and men, and the nine worlds not come to an end.

Fast did the wolf grow in strength and in hunger; his fierceness did grow twice as fast. Heimdall and Thor were loath to approach him, Frey and Freya were too. White fangs like longswords and jaws a full shield broad, none but the bravest dared feed him. Tyr the sword-thane, the oath-strong alone, would brave the fangs of the beast. Day upon day he fed the war wolf; day upon day did he strengthen.

Fenris on blood and meat grew horse-high, and promised to grow yet beyond. The gods feared his hunger and fierceness yet more. War Wolf they called him, and feared his blood hunger, for the truth was his hunger still grew. No amount of blood and flesh would satisfy him; thus it is with the wolf called War.

First taken and bound was Garm, Fenris's pup, taken and chained at Hel's gate. Garm to guard his aunt's corpse-gate, that none but the dead may it pass. Then chains were forged by the dwarves of the hills, chains forged of steel of Muspelheim. Fenris was dared by Thor and by Tyr to test his strength against this chain. A chain forged of the hardest steel under earth, a steel as strong as the mountains! Fenris then howled and hurled his great bulk, and shattered the chain, and chewed its lengths into splinters. Great was the fear of the ravening wolf, his hunger and terrible power.

Dromi, a new chain, was forged of so heavy a link that only great Thor could yet lift it. Spells of the dwarf lore, the magic of thought, sought to bind the wolf hunger with iron.

Again to Fenris they offered the challenge, to test his strength against the fetter. The wolf took the

challenge with a joyous wolf howl, sure that his strength was the better. With a howl the War Wolf did shatter his bonds. With its breaking came a whisper of knowledge.

At the roots of the Tree did the Norns keep the wells. Well did they read what was written. The wolf would devour the Victory Father; Fenris would slay him by fang. Vidar the Silent would take his blood price, but the Twilight would come at his passing.

The price of his freedom was doom for the world, for free did Fenris bring Twilight. Twilight, the death of the world and of men, would fall with the Victory-Father.

Freya was the wisest of all of the women; Odin, the wisest of men. The mysteries and magics of all of their craft were joined with the dwarves for a binding. Gleipnir, called the Entangler, forged for the binding of Fenris. Forged from the noise of a cat walking, woman's beard, mountain roots, bear sinew, fish scale and bird spittle, Gleipnir fluttered like a ribbon of silk. Borne by Skirnir, Frey's good shield man, did Gleipnir come to the Aesir.

Wary of tricks did the wolf eye the bond, so slender it was naught but a ribbon. "What honour," he said, "What glory have I, from breaking so slender a tether?" The gods teased the wolf for fearing such a cord, where his strength had scoffed at strong iron, but the Wolf of War smelled a trap in the wind; the son of the Deceiver smelled cunning.

"A bargain I'll make to my Aesir kinsmen. I'll lie myself down for the binding, if one of the strong sons of Odin will place his own right hand here in my muzzle."

Thor with his glove for his hammer did quail; Heimdall the watcher grew wary. Tyr the sword-thane alone held his courage. Tyr held his honour most high.

He who fed the wolf from his hand, strode forward with sword hand held high.

"I swear by my name I will give you my hand, and leave it while you test your fetter."

The wolf barked his laugh, and lay himself down, while Skirnir did bind him with a collar. On the island of Lyngvi, far from both man and god, they bound the wolf with Gleipnir the Entangler. Tyr stood with sword hand between the white fangs while Frey's man locked on Gleipnir. Fenris rose with a bound to his feet, and hurled his great strength against the binding. Pull as he might he could not break this bond; writhe as he might he could not slip it. Bound hard at last until the end of the days, Fenris was chained on his island. He threw back his head and howled his fury, howled his hatred and ravening hunger. While he howled Tyr's hand was free to withdraw, the sword hand was free of its prison.

Best of the swordsmen in all Aesir halls, the champion of duel and of honour, Tyr watched his sword hand as it sat on the fangs, and O! how he longed to withdraw it.

Meeting the eye of Fenris himself, Tyr gazed at his mindless blood hunger. His sword or his word he would break on this day, the sword-thane and oath-strong did ponder.

Fenris remembered a hostage he had, and feared in his rage he would lose him. Tyr made no move to recover his hand, and instead stood unmoved right beside him. With a howl of rage he snarled to his keeper, with a cry took the hand that would feed him.

"Honour, not sword hand, is the mark of the warrior," did Tyr to the wolf now avow. Pride was in his stance as he held up his stump.

"Thus is my honour remembered."

Garm at Hel's gate did hear his dread father's cry, and swear his own oath of vengeance. To slay the Wolf-Binder swore the son of the wolf, but the Norns knew he would fall in the doing.

From now to the end will the fetters yet hold, and chain the dread wolves in their hunger. Tyr the sword thane, the oath-strong did decide that with his hand he would serve honour and people. Let the folk now hearken to the Wolf and the Word, and the price to bind the one with the other.

Snjóa

by Freydis Heimdallson

Once upon a time, far to the north of the lands of our ancestors, there lived a rich jarl.

Many men followed him, and he had many of the tough little horses that lived so well in the cold and barren lands. He had a good, strong wife who led well and had borne him several fine children. But one of his proudest possessions was his axe.

No tool for chopping wood, this; it was a fine bearded war axe worthy of a jarl of his stature. It had been gifted to his father's father's father, many long years before, and had served the family well in times of need ever since.

Unfortunately, one day, as he and his men fought a fierce bear that had lost its fear of men and taken to raiding the holdings, he struck the beast such a blow that the axe broke. The bear's skull broke too, but that was little consolation. No man around had the skill to repair such a fine weapon. One man could make it as strong as it had been, but not as beautiful; the one who had the skill to make it as beautiful as it had been could do so only by sacrificing its strength. All feared it to be as dead as the bear.

The bear was skinned and its meat not wasted; all summer long the jarl gazed at the thick fur and mourned the loss of his axe.

Finally, though, a solution presented itself. There were dwarves, sons of Ymir, dwelling only a few days' ride to the south. Perhaps, it was suggested, they might be persuaded to repair the axe? Everyone knew there were no smiths like Dvalin's kin; surely if the axe could be repaired, the forgers of Thor's hammer and Freya's necklace could do it, although the price was likely to be high.

50

Expensive it would be, the jarl was sure, for the dwarves are known for their lust for gold as much as for their craftsmanship; nevertheless he entrusted the oiled remains of his axe, carefully wrapped, to his most trusted retainer, to see if the dwarves would repair it, and what they would ask. A prince's ransom was sent along with him to sweeten his words, and a week later the man returned, triumphant. The cost would be high, but the axe would be delivered to a certain spot in a month's time, stronger and more beautiful than any the hands of men could ever hope to forge.

The jarl was ecstatic. He cared little for the cost; he knew a summer's raiding would bring it back to him again, if he fared boldly. Eagerly he paced away the month until the axe would be ready.

Finally the time came. He saddled his favourite horse, loaded a second animal with the rest of his payment, and called his favourite hound. His youngest daughter he took with him as well; she was a bright and cheerful child, and the journey would be a grand adventure for her. His huskarls objected strenuously to being left behind, but he refused their company, saying he was no sheep to ride in a flock, and while there were few enough bandits in the area, he did not want to attract unwanted attention by riding with a large retinue. "Besides," he said, "Too great a display and the dwarves may find my axe-geld too low. Better I ride as a simple man with his child than as a great one with his warriors."

And off he rode, with only his daughter for company.

Long as the summer's days are in those far northlands, still the shadows were lengthening when they finally stopped to make camp, in a little copse against a hill. They gathered wood, cooked their dinner over a small fire, and rolled in their cloaks to sleep, trusting to the dog, Veiðihundur, to alert them to danger.

However, as far as they had ridden, so far had Veiðihundur run, panting joyfully beside the horses, and he slept so soundly that he never noticed the men creeping silently through the trees until they leapt upon the jarl.

Roused from sleep to find himself already under attack, the jarl knew he had no hope; his life was forfeit, the price of the treasure he carried. However, he fought on, with every weapon at his disposal, dirt and rocks and finally, staggering to his feet and roaring, his sword, while the dog leapt and bit. He would not make the theft easy for them; but more importantly, he hoped to keep them distracted and buy time for his daughter to make her escape.

Small as she was, the bandits had not noticed her lying in the shadows of the wood for the fire. Fearing for her father, but knowing she could do nothing but give his death meaning with her life, she inched her way clear of the battle, into the shadow of the trees.

From their shelter, she watched as long as she dared before turning and fleeing into the wood. Stumbling in the darkness, she finally found a hollow beneath a fallen log just of a size for her to squeeze into. She spent the rest of the night there, cold and grief-stricken, listening to the distant squabbling of the bandits as they searched their baggage, until, as false dawn lightened the sky, Veiðihundur, bruised and battered, and grieving as she, found his way to her. It wasn't hard to persuade him to squeeze in beside her, and his comforting bulk helped warm her even as his fur soaked up her tears.

They stayed there until she had heard nothing of the bandits for several hours, then they slowly and carefully made their way back.

The little camp was ruined. Their neatly stacked wood was scattered across the clearing, as were those few belongings the bandits had had no use for. Most of the food had been taken as well; only a few crusts of bread remained, trampled to uselessness in the dirt.

She tried not to look at the torn heap that had been her father, but she noted with pride just how they had had to hew him to make the mighty jarl fall as she rolled him onto his back. His sword they had taken, so she fashioned him one out of branches, and gently closed his hands around that before covering him with rocks.

By the time she had finished his simple barrow, the shadows were again lengthening. Their little fire pit beckoned, promising safety, but she knew it for a lie; the light might attract the bandits, who would come looking to see what other valuables they might have missed, and her poor dear father was nothing but meat now, so far as animals' noses were concerned. She dared not stay.

Instead, she and the dog spent another night in the shelter of the log, listening to each other's stomachs growl.

The next morning she and Veiðihundur went the other way, to a small creek they had passed on their journey. Barely a trickle it was, but it was more than enough to slake their thirst. The girl had some wood craft, and knew plants with which to fill her belly. The dog turned up some mushrooms. She did not trust them, being wise enough to know better than to eat one she did not know, but Veiðihundur happily devoured them and nosed under the moss for more.

What was she to do? Surely her father's men would come looking for them when they did not return, but they would not be expected back for several more days, and it might be even longer before they realised that she and her father were missing, and not simply delayed. By the time they arrived, she might have already long been warming the belly of a wolf. If she walked home she would meet the men the sooner; she might even arrive before they left. But she had no water skin, and what had taken only a day to ride would take many more on foot. And the wolves, four-footed and two, would find her as easily on the move as standing still. Besides, she was not certain she remembered the way.

She finally decided to stay with the creek. She knew that even if she ate not another bite before her father's men arrived, still she would survive the fortnight, and a fortnight again, so long as she had water. Besides, where there was water there would be game; if she teased a few threads loose from the hem of her cloak she might be able to braid them into a snare, and catch a rabbit or a squirrel for her and Veiðihundur to gnaw. She had no way to make a fire, but meat was meat, and the cloak and the dog would keep her warm enough at night, if she could find shelter to keep them safe.

That night she spent, sleepless and cold, in the safety of the high branches of a tree, while Veiðihundur paced and whined below, unable to follow her up. The next morning, after breaking their fast as best as they could, the two set off to find more accommodating shelter.

And so it was that she was living, she and Veiðihundur, in the shelter of some large boulders made snug with branches and grass, when they were finally found, almost a month later.

However, it was not her father's men who came across them, skinny and dirty and matted the pair of them. Luckily, it was not the bandits, either.

It was the dwarves.

She gathered, listening to them as they coaxed her out with bread and good meat, that they had waited for some time for her father to arrive, before deciding to go and find him and their payment

58

themselves. From the remains of their camp, the dwarves had had a pretty good idea of what had happened to their payment; they had stumbled upon her as they made their way home again.

Dwarves, it is said, prize gold above all else, and this may very well be true, but that does not make them heartless. The child, barely taller than they themselves, was lost and starving. They had no one to spare to see her home, even if she could have made the trip (for dwarves do not ride), and although the jarl was dead, still they had repaired his axe as agreed. Gold and jewels he had promised them; and here was his daughter, with gold in her hair, and sapphires in her bright, wild eyes; they would see no other payment from him, that much was obvious, and if they took her in as payment then she would at least be cared for.

And so the daughter of the jarl and his dog went to live with the dwarves.

Dwarves are a hardy lot, small, but doughty; and although she quickly outgrew them, she was hard-pressed to keep up with them. Wood they needed for the forges, deep in the secret belly of the earth, but what a dwarf would haul in a few minutes would take her an hour. Buckets of water she would haul to keep the barrels topped up; she would struggle with one where a dwarf would carry two with ease. But she did not give up, but worked to keep up as best as she could, and grew the stronger for it. She was not unmindful of the debt she owed to them, and earned her keep and Veiðihundur's readily, and did not complain.

In fact, she rarely spoke a word at all. The grief of her father's death, and the hardship of the following weeks had stilled her tongue; they would have thought her entirely dumb did they not sometimes hear her talking quietly to Veiðihundur as she ruffled his fur. They never did learn her name, and so they named her anew themselves, for the paleness of her skin, and her silence. *Snjóa*, they called her, which in the language of those lands meant *Snow*.

And so Snjóa grew taller and stronger, as Veiðihundur grew old and toothless. As the axe was paid for with her own existence, and she the only one there who could claim it, it was passed to her; the dwarves, seeing no point in a weapon unused, taught her to use it, for they themselves prefer axes over other weapons.

And finally the day came when it was agreed that she was a child no longer, but a young woman, and she was released from her bondage.

She had not considered it so; she thought full bellies and the warmth of the forge for her and Veiðihundur a fine exchange for her labour, but dwarves do not usually keep thralls, and they judged that she had repaid her father's debt to them. Accordingly, while she was welcome to stay, she was also free to leave. They built her a small hof not far from their caverns, and the fresh air and sun was a powerful lure. However, each winter, 'Snjóa' or not, when the sun stayed behind the mountains anyway, and the cold crept in with bitter teeth, she would return to the warmth and the light of the forge, far below the glittering snow.

Some time passed in this way, before, one summer, something astonishing happened. In those wild lands, far from the dwellings of men, she saw, for the first time in years, another human.

Sigurd was himself the son of a jarl, and a keen hunter; he had pursued a particularly fine buck for many miles, outlasting his men and hounds, driving deep into the wild woods where men did not often dare to go. You can imagine his wonder, therefore, when he looked up from the stream in which he and his horse had slaked their thirst, to see a young woman staring at him in shock!

And such a woman! To call her beautiful was to

not do her justice, he thought; she stood for only a

moment before turning and fleeing, but the image of her was burned into his eyes: tall, and slender, with eyes like sapphires against the shining gold of her hair. Almost he thought Freya herself had he seen, but no goddess ever left footprints in the soft earth of a stream bank, he reasoned. But by the time he had dragged his horse from the water and mounted, she was gone.

Thoughtfully he made his way back to his camp, and said little until his father, the jarl, called for the tale of the end of the hunt as they roasted the fine venison over the fire. Astounded, the others listened to the tale, and while some were inclined to warn him away from what might be a dangerous wight, none could fault his logic that only a human foot would leave human footprints. They were hunters, after all.

Sigurd resolved to return and find the maiden again as soon as he could, but young men have duties; the sons of jarls more so than most. The place where they camped was several days' ride from his father's holdings, and the stream where he had seen her the better part of a day's fast ride past that, and it would be long and long before he would have so much time to himself again. In the meantime, he talked of her when he could, and dreamed of her when he could not.

Most of the rest of his people simply teased the love-sick young man, or rolled their eyes behind his back, but there was one who grew sick herself at his words. The daughter of a wise woman, she herself had a certain standing in the community, and had always regarded Sigurd as hers. Was she not comely herself, with her dark hair and emerald eyes? Was she not of a suitable age? She had assumed, as had others, that Sigurd would some day turn to her; his words about the mysterious maiden burned and gnawed at her breast until she could stand it no longer.

Magics she had learned from her mother, and from others besides, and not all were good. Many poisons she knew, and ways to bring madness, as well as how to bring down a fever, or to set an arm to heal straight.

With care, then, she baked a loaf of bread, and cooked meat, and set off to find the strange maiden herself.

It was many days' journey, through strange lands she had not before seen, but finally she arrived at a place she thought must be where Sigurd had seen the unearthly maiden. The traces of his horse's passage were scant, but she found, in that lonely spot so far from human habitation, the delicate marks of dainty shod feet in the softer earth near the stream, and the marks were not old. She therefore found a likely spot in the sun, and unbinding her hair, began to comb it, and sing.

Some might have called it magic, for magics can be wrought with the binding and unbinding of hair by those who know the secret ways, but the only magic she called up that day was that of curiosity. By the footprints in the bank, the woman she sought came here often; Maegelwyn (for that was her name) hoped she might hear her voice, and be drawn to her by simple curiosity.

And so it came to pass. Snjóa had not brought Veiðihundur with her, for despite the late summer warmth, his old bones creaked and pained him, so she had no warning from the dog. But her own ears were sharp, as sharp as any who live in the quiet woods, and she wondered greatly at the strange voice she heard piping in the distance, blending with the chuckle of the creek, so unlike the deep rough voices of the dwarves.

Cautiously she crept closer to see what manner of creature sang with such a voice; but for all her woodcraft, Maegelwyn perceived her, one way or another, and smiled to herself.

"Hello!" she called gaily. "I had not thought to meet another in such a lonely spot! Please, won't you share your company and my lunch with me?"

Hesitantly Snjóa stepped forward. "Who are you?" she asked. "And whence did you come?"

The witch laughed, a pretty tinkling sound. "My name is Süka, and I came whence all men come. Will you sit and eat with me? The sun is warm, and I have enough bread and meat for two."

Snjóa did not trust the strange woman, but Süka had given her no reason to be rude, so she carefully sat a little distance away. However, she was careful; dwarves are straightforward creatures who see no reason to lie about anything, and something in her manner rang false to Snjóa's ears. So she accepted the meat and bread with thanks, but only pretended to nibble it. She did not trust Süka's hearty bites; the stranger watched her too closely from the sides of her eyes.

At last the bread and meat was gone; Süka devouring hers, Snjóa crumbling hers into pieces that she dropped behind the log upon which she was sitting, when Süka seemed inattentive.

Süka stood and swept the crumbs from her skirt; Snjóa did the same. "Thank you for sharing your lunch, Süka," she said politely.

"And thank you for your company!" the witch replied. "I had best be on my way now; I don't want to be wandering in the dark!" And with a wave she was off.

Snjóa watched her leave with narrowed eyes; there was no place but the dwarves' hearths and her own home that could be reached on foot before dark. She misliked the woman, for all that she spoke fair.

As for Maegelwyn, she skipped away through the woods, but stopped where she knew she could not be seen, and waited. The potion she had used to poison half the meat and bread caused a swift death, but it was painful; she waited to hear her rival cry out in agony as she died.

But no cry did she hear. Softly, carefully, she crept back to where she could see the place they had lunched without being seen. To her bitter rage, Snjóa was neither dead nor writhing in agony, but merely sitting quietly, staring intently at something on the ground.

The witch could only assume that she was somehow immune to the poison; she vowed to return, and left to start the long journey home.

Snjóa, for her part, was staring at the body of a little bird. It had hopped down for the crumbs as soon as Süka left, but after eating its fill, the poor little thing writhed and fell over, quite dead.

Snjóa knew nothing of poisons, nor why anyone would have tried to hurt her, but she guessed that the strange woman meant her harm. She filled the bucket she had brought with water, as she had come to do, and left for home, frowning thoughtfully.

It was not quite a fortnight before Snjóa came across the woman again, once more sitting on the log in the sunny spot. Süka greeted her gaily; Snjóa forced a smile in return. She still did not know why the woman wished her harm, and had been unable to answer that riddle, but she was determined to avoid the harm nonetheless.

Süka had no bread or meat with her this time, but once again her long black hair was unbound; she was combing her raven tresses with a gaily painted wooden comb.

"How pretty!" Snjóa exclaimed. She herself combed her hair in the manner of the dwarves, with her fingers.

"Do you like it?" asked Süka. "Here, try it if you like."

Snjóa did not trust the woman, and was wary of any gift from her, but thought that if she had been able to comb her own hair with it, she herself might take no harm from doing the same. She was not surprised, however, when the touch of the wood awoke an unpleasant, prickly numbness in her fingers. Still, Süka had held it without harm, so Snjóa accepted it, and lightly made a few passes through her own unbound hair with it.

"Oh, how pretty the colours shine against your hair!" exclaimed Süka, clapping her hands like a child. "You must keep it! No, I have plenty more at home, and that yellow has never looked half as lovely against my own hair." And she insisted that Snjóa keep the comb, even offering to show how it could be used to pin her hair back out of the way.

Snjóa allowed her to do so, but readjusted it so it no longer pressed against her scalp as soon as Süka let go; she trusted the prickly numbness against her scalp no more than she did against her fingers.

72

Once more, with a smile and a wave Süka left; as soon as she was out of sight Snjóa yanked the bright comb from her hair. She wrapped it in a corner of her apron to carry it home to burn; she did not trust that whatever poison or spell was upon it would not leech into the soil or stream and cause mischief if she simply let it lie or buried it.

The comb burned brightly, and with strange colours and a dizzying smoke.

Snjóa began to take her axe with her to the creek.

Maegelwyn hoped that the comb would kill her rival, but after the food had failed to poison her, she did not trust to it. She thought it best that she return a third time, to make sure of things. One more poisoned trap she prepared, and at earliest light, off she stole, away from the stedding.

However, Sigurd had noticed her lengthy absences, and did not trust them. So when he saw her quietly leading a horse away, he swiftly saddled his own, and followed.

For several days he trailed her, always staying out of sight, tracking her rather than following by sight. He was not pleased to find her following the way his own hunt had gone; by the grim set of her jaw as she had left he guessed that her purpose was to seek the strange maiden, and that her intentions were not good. But he couldn't stop his heart from leaping at the thought that he might once again see the mysterious lady.

After many days, Maegelwyn stopped in a small clearing. She tied her horse to a tree; by the way it settled down to eat the grain she poured out for it, Sigurd guessed that she had done this several times before. When she stepped away through the woods, he tied his own horse beside hers, and stealthily followed.

Snjóa was not surprised to find Süka waiting for her at the log again. She had been expecting her for some time. The woman seemed to want her dead, although Snjóa could not fathom why, and she guessed that Süka would keep appearing until she accomplished her task. This time, she was idly twirling a strange, bright flower between her fingers. "Ah, my friend!" she called to Snjóa when she saw her. "Come and see what I have here! The perfume of this flower is the rarest and loveliest in the world; it is said that one has but to smell its scent once to know what true beauty is. Come and have a sniff!"

As Sigurd crept closer he heard voices; hiding in the trees he recognized the stream where he had once glimpsed the maiden. He saw her again now, her clear strong voice carrying to him across the water.

" 'Friend' you name me," she said to Maegelwyn, seated on a log before her, "And yet twice already you have tried to harm me. 'Friend' you name me, when you shared with me poisoned meat and bread, and gifted me with a poisoned comb. I do not trust your friendship, Süka, and I think that before I inhale the vapours of your flower, you had better do so yourself."

Maegelwyn's voice was silky. "Poisoned food? Poisoned combs? I do not know what you mean, dear friend. You saw me eat from the same loaf, from the same meat; I used the comb myself before I gifted it to you. Your words hurt me, sister."

"You ate the same food as I without harm, Süka, and yet, only one end of a snake is dangerous. Smell the flower."

"Sister mine—"

"Name me not sister until you smell the flower yourself."

Maegelwyn rose with a sneer. "I will not stand here and be insulted by one to whom I gifted my own comb and shared my own food. If you wish to reject this gift—"

The pale woman raised an axe, a weapon fit for a jarl. "Breathe the scent, or breathe your last."

The witch paled. "Dear friend—"

"The flower or the axe!" the woman barked. "Choose!" And she shifted into what Sigurd recognised as a battle stance.

Hesitantly, Maegelwyn raised a brightly-coloured flower to her face. Slowly, carefully, as though she were approaching a snake, she buried her nose in it. Staring at her rival, she inhaled deeply.

Snjóa could smell no scent from the flower, but Süka breathed deep, staring hard at her. Then, without a sound, her eyes drifted closed and she fell to the ground, the flower falling from her lifeless hand.

Sighing, Snjóa lowered her father's axe and sat on the log, unable to take her eyes from the crumpled form before her. She felt numb; she didn't even startle when a man stepped out of the woods and splashed across the little creek.

"She's dead," she told him. "She's dead, and I don't even know why she was trying to kill me."

He knelt before her. "She was trying to kill you because she thought to wed me, and I could speak of no one but you."

"Me? But how do you know *me*?"

And finally raising her eyes to his, she recognised the handsome young man she had been startled to see in this very spot, so many months ago.

"Lady, what is your name?"

She blinked at him. "Snjóa, the dwarves call me."

"And what does your family call you?"

"Mjallhvít Eiriksdottir, I was named when I lived in the lands of men."

"Then, Mjallhvít Eiriksdottir, will you come with me once more to the lands of men, and live with me as my wife?"

And so it came to pass. The dwarves gifted her a generous dowry; she used a portion of it to pay the wergild for Maegelwyn's death, so her mother did not become her enemy. And while Sigurd's father was unhappy with his lengthy and unannounced absence, he could not complain of his son's choice of brides, especially once he learned who her father had been.

And when their oldest son was of age, she gifted him his grandfather's axe, and fostered him with the dwarves, who taught him as they had taught her; he grew up to be a renowned warrior, who brought honour, wealth, and fame to both his parents' houses.

Draugr of Hudiksvall

By John Mainer

Not far from Uppsala in the land of the Swede was the village of Hudiksvall. Outside the village were the farms and halls, flocks and fields that fed the village, and along the windswept shore were the halls and homes of the fishermen, and others who looked to the sea for their fortune.

One such home was set into a small hillside, its rough-hewn timbers well-chinked against the sea wind, and whose stout sod roof grazed all manner of fractious goats and rampaging chickens and children. This was Hrolfsteadding, or the steading of Hrolf, and although well-founded and fallow, it was alone on the shore, for alone of Hudiksvall would Hrolf brave the Draugr of the point.

Draugr are barrow-wights, the spirits of those kings or their carls who sleep in their barrow mound, unwilling to give up the guard of the treasures they won in life. No-one recalled the saga of the nameless king whose barrow stood alone against the point; was he some great king who was buried beneath the keel of his favourite ship along the shore he once defended? Hrolf thought him some red-handed sea raider who fell not to blade, but to age and time. Unbeaten in his life, the treasures he won by his dread blade he guarded still, and the ship that carried him outward now crouched over his grave like a sleeping dragon. Since Hrolf brought back both the gold and wife to found his steading from such a voyage, he thought the site a lucky one.

In the manner of such things, as the hall rose, so did his wife's belly, and soon the song of hammer and adze were joined with the sounds of children, as Hrolf and his Astrid saw their kindred increase. As the children grew, so did Hrolf's restlessness, and soon the men of the village were asking Hrolf to lead them in an expedition of their own, leaving Astrid and the children in the steading alone. After blot to Odin and the Aesir for luck in battle and Njord for fortune, Hrolf waded out into the waters and poured a horn of his own brewed mead to black Ran of the deeps, and another to the nameless sea king whose barrow showed the richness he sought to match.

Astrid would sew by the firelight while her husband would enthral the children with his tales of adventure, of gods and heroes, monsters and magic. By the time Hrolf was ready to go a-viking again, his son Vali was filled with tales of daring, and his daughter Thorgerd with the wisdom of their lessons. Hrolf had no fear with his dear Astrid to watch over them, but Astrid herself was much in demand. When birthing was hard of babies or herds, Astrid was called the breadth of Hudksvall. One such birth held Astrid for two full nights, and left young Vali with time to watch the goats, and dream of the Sea King's Barrow.

"With a sword like the Sea King's I could be a great warrior!" Vali said.

Thorgerd shook her head and tried to restrain him. "It's probably cursed, and rusted by the sea air. Besides, Father won *his* sword and mail from someone who thought they made him a hero. Father still laughs at the telling."

Boys are like goats (hence they make decent herders): once they get a bad idea in their head, they won't let it go. When Thorgerd went to sleep that night, Vali crept out, slipping down the strand to the Sea King's barrow, ready to make his legend, ready to seize his blade, his fortune, and his place in the sagas. Using a shovel with a real iron edge, he dug his way through the sod and stone of the mound. The wood of the hull was thick and strong, but the roots of the scrub trees had breached it, leaving a hole he could widen. Like an otter he wiggled and dug, till a path he had made. With his torch he beheld the wonder of the barrow.

The Sea King rested on a bed of crossed spears. His flesh had long rotted, leaving a mail-clad skeleton clutching a sword to his chest. Golden rings bound his arms, and silver chains and broaches tarnished to black hinted at the rich cloaks and furs that once covered him, but Vali's eyes were only for the blade. It took him two hands to lift it, and the wooden and leather sheath cracked to splinters when he drew it forth. Striking a pose, he rested the broad point on the rusted byrnie of the sleeping king.

"I am Vali, son of Hrolf, conqueror of the Sea King!"

His voice rang light and brassy in the dank earth, and the barrow began to grow chill. Vali shivered as he felt the cold touch of fear. He began to walk back to the hall, but began to run when he saw blue barrow-light dance over the barrow, and heard the dry rasp of the wind, like the sound of old bones grinding together. He hoped it was the wind, because a part of him thought it sounded like a voice colder than ice rasping his name.

When Vali burst into the hall, slamming the great door and setting the bar behind him, Thorgerd woke instantly. So did her twin brothers, who began crying immediately. When Thorgerd had the little toddlers bundled back up, she looked to see her trembling brother covered with dirt (not unusual), and clutching a sword larger than his leg (not usual). Just then the great door slammed back against the bar, and a rasping voice like an axe dragged along stone called out.

"You took my sword! You struck Vajbjorn the Grim; no man may do so and live!

"I will take your head, and burn your hall, and nail your thieving hands to the barn door for the ravens to pick clean!"

With each threat the Sea King's hands hammered the door, and the stout timbers began to crack, the leather of the hinges and iron of the nails to creak and strain. Thorgerd looked from her sobbing brother, to the crying twins, and knew they would not see the dawn if the Sea King kept coming.

"You have to help me!" begged Vali, his bravado shattered by the sight of knuckle bones peeking through the door frame.

"Quiet!" shouted Thorgerd, thinking fiercely.

Father had told them of draugr and spirits, warnings her brother had clearly ignored.

She ran to the kitchen, and took the salt chest that was her mother's treasure, her own small horn, and the light axe her father had gifted Vali with at Yule. She turned to Vali and told him her plan.

"You will slip out the smoke hole and run down the strand. You will let him see you when you are between the barrow and the hall," she said sternly.

"He will kill me!" wailed Vali.

"He will kill us all, and burn the hall, if we do nothing!" Thorgerd said. "All you must do is reach the shore. Get to the water and he will not harm you. Remember what father said," Thorgerd whispered.

Reminded of the old tale, the children whispered their father's words together: "Ran is jealous, and keeps what is hers. She harvests men with her nets, and no one she takes can return. Salt is Ran's blood, and the dead know to fear it. No draugr can pass it, nor stand its touch, lest Black Ran take what is hers."

"I cannot stay in the sea forever; it is cold," Vali said, thinking at last.

"By dawn this will end, or Sunna's first touch will send this Vajbjorn to Hel. Sunna's touch is life, and burns all unclean. Hella will hold him 'till Ragnarok, or father comes home," stated Thorgerd confidently.

The door was sagging and showed more gaps than Vajbjorn's ribcage by the time that Vali called to the draugr.

"Vajbjorn the Blind, I'm here behind you! Can you catch me with those moss-covered knees?" Vali laughed, his humour and courage restored with Thorgerd's plan.

"Thief, I will have your skull for my dice cup!" the draugr rasped as he lumbered towards the running boy.

Salt chest under one arm, axe at her belt, and sword braced against her shoulder, Thorgerd eased her way out the shattered door, and headed for the barrow. Working swiftly, she scraped a trench with the axe in the barrow's mouth. She spread the coarse salt in a thick line inside the trench, testing to make sure it had no breaks, and wary that the trench kept it from the treacherous sea wind. The sword she stood point down before her. When she was ready, she raised and sounded her little horn.

Not the raw challenge of her father's war horn, it was the call that told the children to come for dinner, the goats to return to the stedding. Trying to muster the bravado her father put in his war horn when he sounded the challenge, she blew and blew, until Vajbjorn and Vali heard her.

Winded as the horn, she took a moment before she called to Vajbjorn.

"Great king, unconquered champion, we have wronged you, and would pay weregild!" She offered in a voice of iron calm and reason.

"Kin of thieves will die as thieves!" Vajbjorn roared. "I take what I want, and gold will not buy your lives." His great spear in his hand, he tottered to the barrow mound. He pulled back the dread spear and howled when he felt the sea salt barring his way.

"My grave, you have taken my grave! Why should I not loose my spear and lay you in my doorstep!" He raved while Thorgerd stood firm.

"Killing me will leave you outside your barrow come the dawn. You cannot reach my brother in Ran's waves, nor your barrow behind her salts. Sunna comes swift with the brightening sky, and I would treat with you, great Vajbjorn." As she had seen her mother stand unflinching

before her father's wrath, so did she stand before Vajbjorn.

A rasping gurgle rumbled slowly into a laugh like shields slamming together.

"Kings and chieftains have cowered before me, bears slinked from my path, and I am defied by a girl child. Had I met you in life, we would be bargaining for your hand, not my suffering price. Very well, state your terms."

"The sword that was stolen returned to you. The axe of your foeman for your spoils. As one blow was struck you with the blade flat, so will you strike one in return. Upon your honour will it be no harder." Thorgerd spoke swiftly, fearing that her courage would fail in the face of his eyeless gaze.

"My honour was tainted when that sprat claimed victory," he rasped, almost joking.

Thorgerd raised up her hands, placing them upon the hilt of the stolen sword.

"By the All-father, before the gods, the spirits of my hearth, and upon the name of my mother, I swear that I will come at every moon and raise a horn to your glory, telling of your might and justice. I swear that your grave mound will be kept as long as our descendants live in Hudiksvall."

With Sunna brightening the horizon, and a soaked and shivering Vali watching from the shore, Vajbjorn considered.

Where he had never trusted the oaths of men, the greed he knew well of old, the iron calm of this girl-child touched him. Speaking slowly, as if remembering the man that he once was, not the draugr he had allowed himself to become, he spoke his judgement.

"The weregild is thus: remember my name at each moon: Vajbjorn the shield-breaker, serpent-rider, Pict-slayer and horse-breaker. I will be buried with the boy-child's axe, and a lock of your hair.

" Vali will have the sword from my hand. A sea wolf's blade should not moulder in the mound. An arm ring of gold will you have for your arm, for the bride-price I would have paid you."

He rose his full height and stared at the sea; he seemed to ignore the dawn that stole upon him. As the sword was passed from girl, to draugr, to boy, Vajbjorn seemed to come alive.

"Sixty sea wolves I once led upon the waves. Will you two follow me now? I sent a thousand men to Ran's black deeps, and full many a comrade as well. Now I go to her whom I loved in my life. To Ran."

Thus did Vajbjorn come to his end; striding swiftly into the sea, a shivering boy-child with sword in two hands, and a spear-straight young maiden beside him.

Until the fall of the temple at Uppsala, the oath was kept upon each moon, across so many generations the truth of the custom became lost.

Gifts

By Freydis Heimdallson

A long time ago, in a land far, far away, in a house in a field on a cliff above the wild tossing sea, there lived a boy named Karl.

His home was far in the Northlands, where the sun hardly went down at all, all summer long; but where the winter nights were cold, and bitter, and endless.

One bright Fall morning, when the sun still peeped above the mountains about the stedding, Karl took his bow, and his knife, and went for a walk. Across the fields about the farm he went, and out towards the wild reaches at the edges, where he might find a nice fat rabbit or a deer for the pot.

He hadn't gone very far at all, though, when suddenly he heard a little tiny voice calling, "Help! Help! Oh, please, somebody, help me!"

Karl stopped and listened. "Who on earth can that be?" he wondered. The next farm was a day's journey away, and there was nothing to the south but wild tossing seas, and nothing to the north but cold and ice and mountains, and nothing east or west but jumbled rocks up the sides of the valley. "Is it a landvaettir, one of the spirits of the rocks and trees?" he wondered. "Or perhaps it is a troll, trying to lure me away to where he can pounce on me and eat me up?" Karl shivered, and was about to turn away, when the voice called again, a little tiny, high voice. "Please, please, somebody help me!"

Karl thought hard for a moment. "If that is a troll, then it doesn't sound like any troll's voice that I ever heard tell of—and it speaks better. It must be a traveller, or a landvaettir; surely it would only bring me luck to help!"

96

So he went in search of the little voice. And just a little ways away, he came across a prickly, poky bush near some big boulders, with something thrashing about inside it.

Karl carefully pushed the branches aside with the tip of his bow, and there he saw a little baby rabbit, all tangled up in the bush!

"Oh ho!" said Karl. "A wee bunny! There isn't much meat on him, but he might make a nice soup..."

"Oh no, please don't eat me!" cried the little rabbit in fright.

"A talking rabbit!" said Karl in surprise. It was the little voice! "Are you a landvaettir?" he asked, curious.

"No," answered the bunny, "I'm just a little rabbit."

"Well," thought Karl to himself, "A talking rabbit is still pretty special. I'd better help it; it might bring me luck." So he very carefully pulled the branches aside, lifted the baby rabbit out, pulled all the thorns and twigs out of his fur, and gently set him down. "How did you get stuck in the bush?" he asked.

"I was hopping along the boulders up there, and I slipped and fell into the bush," said the little rabbit. "I got all tangled up, and whenever I moved I got poked. It was awful! Thank you for helping me!"

"Well, it's lucky for you that I came along," said Karl. "Would you like me to lift you back up over the rocks?"

"No, thank you," said the little rabbit. "I can climb quite well, usually." He hopped quickly back up to the top of the rocks, *hop, hop, hop*, and poked his head back over. "If you ever need help from a rabbit, just call!" he called down to Karl, and then, with a wave of his paw, he was gone.

Karl laughed. He didn't know how a tiny little rabbit could help someone as big as him! But he was glad to have been able to help, all the same. He picked up his bow and headed back to the stedding. The morning was growing late, and he had chores to do.

Karl didn't tell anyone about his little adventure with the baby rabbit. Either no one would believe him, and would think he was either lying about the rabbit, or they would think that he had gone slightly mad; or, worse, they might believe him after all, and he didn't think it would be good for the rabbit to have everyone clambering about the rocks looking for it. So he said nothing.

Karl didn't see the rabbit again for a very long time. Harvest came, and all the crops were brought in; the wheat was threshed, and ground into flour, and baked into bread, enough bread to last all winter long, they hoped; hay was brought in to feed the animals; meat was salted, and fish was dried... All the food that they had grown all summer long was put away for the winter. Wood and peat was put away for the fires, and every drafty little hole they could find in the walls was plugged with moss and mud. And when the last stalk of wheat had been cut, and the last loaf of bread baked, and the last carrot bundled away, and the last of the meat put down, they had a feast. There was music and light and warmth, and then there was winter.

Winter in the Northlands was very cold, and very dark. The sun barely peeped above the mountains at all, and it was too cold to leave the house unless they had to. Even the animals stayed in their barn. Everyone sat on the long benches that lined the walls of the big long hall, or huddled as close to the smoky little fire as they could, and tried to stave off boredom. They talked, and sang songs, and told tales, and played board games, and carved. They carved everything in sight. Karl took an old cow's horn, and scraped it smooth, and carved it up as a Yule-gift for his father; for his mother he carved a beautiful little comb out of antler, for her lovely long hair. For his little sister Asa he took scraps of fabric and tufts of wool, and made a beautiful little doll. And still the cold crept in, even through the thick sod walls, and the wind howled.

One night (or day, perhaps; it was hard to tell, in the dimness of a home with no windows, and with no sun in the sky beyond the smoke holes), they were woken up by a howling storm. The hof shook as though giants were stomping all around it and hammering on it with their fists, and the wind shrieked as if in anger. And it was so cold that everyone sat as close to the fire as they could, and huddled in their furs, and tried not to shiver.

Finally, after three days, they awoke to silence.

But it almost seemed too quiet. Sound was muffled, as though a giant blanket was thrown over the whole house.

"Well," said Karl's father, "I'd better check on the animals." It had been three days since they could get to the barn to feed them, and the animals would be hungry.

So he put on his nice thick warm boots, and his nice thick warm coat, and his nice thick warm gloves, and his nice thick warm hat, and he opened the door.

But instead of the fields, and the barn, all he could see was white! They were snowed in!

"Oh, no!" everyone cried. "We'll have to dig out." Karl's father started to scoop great armloads of snow down, but, "Stop!" cried their mother. "Hang on a minute! I'm not having my house filled up with snow. Wait a moment." She hurried into the storeroom, and came back with the biggest pot they had, and hung it over the fire. "There," she said; "Put the snow in that."

So Karl's father dug the snow out, and Karl and Asa carried the snow to the great big pot, where it melted into water. All day long they worked.

Now, a lot of snow melts down into a very little bit of water. But they filled the pot with snow many times over, so many times that finally the pot was brimming with snowmelt, and they were all exhausted. But still, there was no sign of sky.

"Come away and warm up," Mother said to Father, closing the door. Karl knew his father was tired, because he didn't argue, but only sat by the fire as close as he could.

"Help me with my boots, Karl," he said; "I can't feel my fingers."

Mother *tsked* as Karl peeled off Father's wet gloves and boots, and helped him out of the coat. All were hung by the fire to dry. "I wish I knew how much further we had to go," Father said, holding out his hands to the fire's warmth. "If it's too deep we might have to dig out through the roof. But if we do that, we won't be able to patch it until Spring…"

Karl sprang to his feet. "I can climb up the rafters and peek out the smoke hole," he said. "Let me have a look and I can see how deep the snow is."

"It might be above the smoke hole," said Father. "The heat from the smoke might have kept it clear, but it might be even deeper than the peak."

"If it is, I'll see that, too," said Karl. "Give me a boost."

Karl climbed onto a bench near the hole at the end of the roof, and then climbed onto his father's shoulders, as Father braced himself against a post. He reached up and grabbed a rafter, and pulled himself up. Very carefully, while his mother wrung her hands below, Karl walked down the rafter to the smoke hole at the peak, and looked out.

There was snow everywhere. It hadn't covered the house, not completely, but if the hole had been large enough for Karl to put his head and shoulders through, he could have reached down and touched it. They had dug barely half way.

"Oh, no!" he said to himself. "We'll have to dig through the roof after all! But if we do that, we'll have a great gaping hole there until Spring, and we may all freeze..!"

Just then, he noticed something moving on the snow. A little something moved, and was still, and then moved again, a little closer. After a moment, he realized that what he was seeing was the shadow of a white rabbit, hopping about on the snow. "Rabbit!" he called. "Rabbit! Do you know of a little baby rabbit that I helped?"

"Yes," said the rabbit, hopping closer, "That was me! Are you all alright in there?"

"Yes," said Karl, "but we can't get out."

"Leave that to me," said the rabbit; "I think I can remember where your door is. Try again in the morning." And the rabbit hopped away.

Very carefully, Karl climbed back down. His family hadn't heard him talking to the rabbit, with his head out the hole; they thought he had just been muttering to himself. "What does it look like?" they asked as he dropped to the floor.

"Bad," said Karl, "But it's not above the peak. Let's try again in the morning."

"All right," said Father, "But what are we going to do with all that water?"

"Well," said Mother, "It's nice and warm. Everyone grab a bowl and a cloth, and we can all have a nice wash. And that will give me enough room to add some vegetables and meat and barley, and make us all a nice hot soup."

So that's what they did. It was nice to get nice and clean again, and with nice fresh water; it took so much snow to melt down that they very rarely all got their own bowl of nice clean water to wash in. And Mother made a lovely soup, and between the one and the other, the pot was emptied.

And all night long, they thought they could hear little scuffling noises outside.

The next morning, Karl's father took his nice thick warm boots, and gloves, and coat, and hat, which were all nice and dry again, after hanging by the fire all night, and put them on. "Right," he said, "Let's get going."

But when he opened the door, to his vast surprise, the tunnel was finished!

Everyone crowded around to see. A tunnel had been dug out, from where Father had stopped the evening before, all the way up to the top of the snow, like a giant rabbit hole. And when they climbed to the top, they could see a similar tunnel to the door of the barn. And when they looked very closely, they could see the marks of little clawed feet in the sides, like rabbit feet.

"I'll help you, Father," said Karl, and went to get his coat.

The animals were very hungry, of course, but otherwise none the worse for wear. As they climbed back up the tunnel out of the barn, Father asked, "Do you know anything about this, Karl?"

"I might," said Karl, hesitant.

"Well, I won't ask about it, if you don't want to tell me," said Father gruffly. "But remember, a gift demands a gift. A favour has been done for us; a favour must be done in return."

"This was the favour in return," said Karl.

"Well, a thank you is always appropriate," said Father, and he went inside.

Karl thought for a little while, and then he went to his mother. "Mother," he asked, "Do you have any rabbit food to spare?"

"Rabbit food? What do you mean?"

"You know," said Karl, "Carrots, beets, that kind of thing."

"Is this about the tunnel?" she asked.

"Yes."

"Then wait here."

She went into the storeroom, and returned a minute later with a bunch of carrots, and half a loaf of bread. "It's all we can spare," she said, "But the carrots are still nice and juicy, and the bread isn't stale at all."

Karl took the food and thanked her, and left it on the snow near the smoke hole, where he had seen the rabbit.

Karl never saw the rabbit again. But all that long winter, whenever they were snowed in too deep for them to dig themselves out, a tunnel would mysteriously appear. And each time, they left food, as much as they could spare. In the Spring they planted extra carrots.

And for the rest of his life, Karl never hunted a rabbit again. A gift demands a gift.

The Story of Mistletoe

By John Mainer

nside the greatest stories are a hundred little stories that get forgotten. In the story of the first winter, the death of Baldur the Bright, there is a story, too, of little Mistletoe. At Yuletide, now, we hang mistletoe, and whenever a boy and girl pass beneath it they must kiss; but so many have forgotten why. The tale of mistletoe is one of love and pride, foolishness and forgiveness.

First and best of the sons of Frigga and Odin was Baldur the Bright. The shining one, his laughter and courage were beacons to the Aesir, and his gentleness the offer of peace when the battle din had faded. Where the world carved by Jottun and Odin from Ymir's bones was cruel and cold, would Baldur add a touch of gentleness and wonder. Where spear-sharp mountain was cut by icy stream would Baldur carve a hidden flowered glen, and softly whispering pool. Where Muspelheim's fire clawed at the ice and rock of earth would Baldur twist and twine them to forge a bubbling spring of warmth to bring the promise of life to the most forsaken fell. When the first war raged between Aesir and Vanir sweet Frigga feared for her son, for ever was he first in battle, and all too swift to offer mercy where death strokes were safer.

In time the Aesir and Vanir swore to peace, and the Vanir too grew to love Baldur. For a time the nine worlds were near peace, the Aesir and Vanir united, the raiding with the Jottun more friendly sport than earnest war. At this time did Frigga vow to make her Baldur safe from harm from all.

To the dwarvish deeps she went, and begged favour of the dwarves: Let not stone or steel, nor metal forged dare harm sweet Baldur's hide. The dwarves looked deep into the secret earth, at the ropes and rivers of gold, the sparkling diamonds promising the wonders of the night sky, and the thousand secret riches that Baldur had woven into the iron deeps when the world was new-forged, and so they swore. To the birds of the air, the beasts of the field, the whales and fishes of the deep did she go and beg safety for bright Baldur, and as each would look to the beauty Baldur had woven into their world, they would promise his protection. From Yggdrasil and all lesser trees did Frigga then beg favour, and one by one they all swore Baldur's weal for the beauty he had given them. At last came Frigga to the youngest of plants, the newborn Mistletoe. She begged protection for her son, and Mistletoe said no.

Mistletoe lives on the oak, and never sees the sun. Far from the ground it sees not beyond the mighty oak's dark leaves. The oak itself did lend its voice to beg and plead with Mistletoe, but Mistletoe had never seen the gifts of Baldur's making. All Frigga's tears and oak's stern words did not move Mistletoe to mercy; in ignorance and pride it swore no oath to the lady mother.

Alone of giant, man, and god, was Loki in his jealousy. Baldur's love meant nothing to him, and he ever sought to mock him. For all his jests did him no good as Baldur never angered, but laughed instead with right good will when Loki's wit did best him. With envy and rage did Loki plot to do fair Baldur evil. At last he thought to ask of Frigga the protection she had won him. In the high feast hall with a gentle smile did Loki come to Frigga.

"How you must fear with such a bold son, that evil must befall him. Of all the gods your Baldur's courage in the vanguard ever finds him."

At Loki's words did Frigga smile, never suspecting evil. She shared with her kinsmen her son's defence, the secrets of his protection.

"The stones of earth, all metals forged, all beasts of water, wind and land have all sworn him protection," did Frigga smile.

Loki pressed for answers. "What of tree and leaf and nut? What of dandelion or rose?"

Frigga laughed at his silly words, and revealed the last of her secret.

"Trees and grasses, bush and vine have all sworn his protection. Only lowly mistletoe of all that lives still dares withhold protection."

Loki laughed and slid away, his mission now completed, sweet Frigga not suspecting yet that Loki plotted treason. Down to Midgard with a silver knife did Loki make his harvest: a slender wand of mistletoe that in the fire with spells he hardened. His arrow forged of mistletoe, and murder in his heart, Loki crossed the rainbow bridge and came to Odin's court.

"A game!" cried Loki, shouting loud; "A sport to test our mettle." Loki's challenge drew every eye and he worked his trick so vile.

"Let Baldur stand before the host, let every warrior try him!" Loath were the gods to raise hand against him, but Baldur did beseech them.

"What harm in this? Let's have a game, let all my friends and brothers try their mightiest of strokes, and let me judge the winner!"

Baldur's words stirred every heart with honest love for battle, and laughing did they all array to try their strokes against him. Odin's spear and Thor's dread hammer, swords of Frey and Heimdall, the bow of Ullr all did fail amidst the warriors' laughter. Blind Hod alone did not take part, until dread Loki urged him on and promised his assistance.

"Come now, brother, what's the harm?" smiled Loki in his treason. "I'll guide your hand upon the bow. Let your warrior's heart remember!"

Hod then smiled and drew his bow, and Loki fit the arrow; dread mistletoe struck Baldur dead and the light of the world fell with him.

All remember what happened next, how sweet Sunna fled from a world without Baldur, how winter came to the world. All remember the punishment of Loki, a binding and torment that would last until the end of days. Each Yule we remember Baldur's arrival at Hel's own hall, how she bade him to sit beside her and join her in her hall until the end of days when he will return to lead the survivors. Who now remembers the fate of Mistletoe, the agent of Baldur's bane?

When Baldur fell, sweet Sunna turned her face away and fled. Without the light of the sun, the world grew cold and dark, the trees lost their leaves, and for the first time Mistletoe saw beyond the embracing arms of oak. Everywhere the dying light showed emptiness and loss, but here and there would beauty shine and Mistletoe did weep. "Who has made this?" would Mistletoe ask at each thing of majesty and wonder. "Baldur," was the answer every time until the heart of Mistletoe was shattered.

Mother Frigga in her rage demanded the death of her son's dread slayer. Of Odin and of Yggdrasil, of Frey and gentle Nerthus she begged the price of mother's vengeance, until every god condemned it. Alone of all the gods did Freya hear the weeping. Alone of all the Vanir did she stoop to hear the reason. To Mistletoe she swiftly flew within her falcon cloak; upon the oak tree did she land beside the weeping plant. The golden goddess softly asked why Mistletoe did weep?

"For Baldur slain, for beauty lost, for love gone out the world."

Freya asked of Mistletoe what wergild would it pay? How could it give back the beauty lost, the love that Baldur offered? When Mother Frigga in her rage came down the Bifrost bridge. Freya stood with Mistletoe to greet the grieving mother.

"Blessed Frigga, will you accept the weregild of the weeping flower? Or will you slaughter and stain the memory of the loving son you've lost?"

Frigga stared hard-eyed and cold to hear the weregild's terms. Mistletoe in humble grief did make this solemn vow:

"Where Yuletide brings the pain of loss will Mistletoe bring love. Beneath my humble leaves let love be now kindled. What fairer grave goods for the sun-bright lord than the promise of love new-kindled? When two now meet beneath my leaves, let love's kiss light between them. Let the light of love remember him that the world weeps for this season."

Now down the ages we remember. Beneath the mistletoe a kiss, the promise of new love, within this coldest season.

Glossary

Some of the terms used in these stories may be unfamiliar to you. Here, then, are a few brief definitions:

Aesir: Odin, Thor, and most of the other Norse Gods and Goddesses

Asgard: The world of the Gods and Goddesses

Barrow: A large mound built over a grave chamber

Blot: An offering to the gods

Dokkalfar: Dark elves, unfriendly to Man

Draugr: An undead body

Fortnight: Two weeks

Hella (also Hel): Norse goddess who keeps the Underworld

Hof: A Norse longhouse

Holdings: The dwellings of men

Huskarl: A household guard

Jarl: A leader of men

Jottun: A Giant

Jottunheim: The land of the Giants

Landvettir: A nature spirit, often of a tree or boulder

Midgard: The world of Men

Muspelheim: The world of Fire and home of the Fire Giants. Ruled by Surt.

Thrall: An indentured servant

Ragnarok: The mythic destruction of Midgard

Ran: Norse goddess of the sea

Stedding: A Norse home, often a farm

Sunna: The Sun; also a goddess

Surt: Ruler of Muspelheim

Symbel: A holy feast

Torc: A type of stiff necklace worn by men

Vanir: Frey and his twin sister Freya, a god and goddess who live with the Aesir in Asgard as hostages to peace

Vinland: North America

Weregild: A fine paid to right a wrong

Wight: An uncanny creature; also a synonym for human.

Wyrd: Fate